KU-246-778

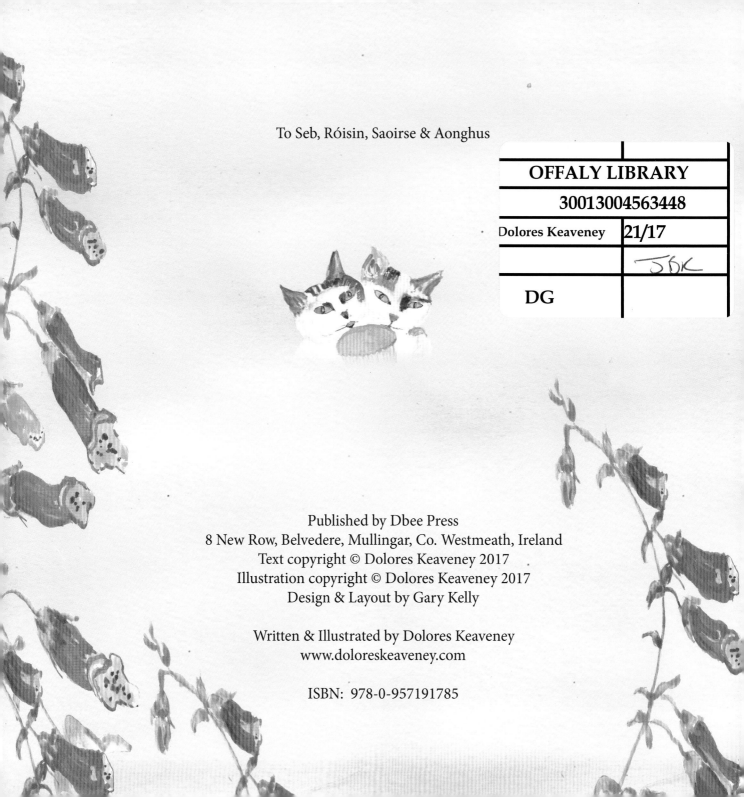

To Seb, Róisin, Saoirse & Aonghus

OFFALY LIBRARY

30013004563448

Dolores Keaveney	21/17
	JDK
DG	

Published by Dbee Press
8 New Row, Belvedere, Mullingar, Co. Westmeath, Ireland
Text copyright © Dolores Keaveney 2017
Illustration copyright © Dolores Keaveney 2017
Design & Layout by Gary Kelly

Written & Illustrated by Dolores Keaveney
www.doloreskeaveney.com

ISBN: 978-0-957191785

Duchess & Valkyrie

Two Little Cats

Duchess and Valkyrie were
two little cats,
That lived in the hay shed
with lots of bats,

They lay in the sun and played in the hay,

And chased all the big rats far far away.

The two little cats
had nowhere to stay,

When their owners decided
to move far away.

Then Grandad offered
to give them a home,

In a small country
cottage where they
could roam.

In the beginning they
were both very shy,

But they got bolder and
bolder as time went by.

They crept into
the house and
ate all the cake.

Grandad realised
he had made
a mistake.

They chased all the birds
and ate all their food,

And this put Grandad in
a terrible mood.

He shouted and chased
them all over the place,

But the two cats just
sat there with a smile on
each face.

'Oh dear',
said Grandad,
'What will I do now',

as he gazed in amazement
while they chased
a big cow.

They ran up the road
and into a house,
And straight up the stairs as
they followed a mouse.

A brown cat called Tommie
gave them a great stare,

So they fled from the
house just like a March hare.

They went up through
the garden as fast
as they could,

Jumped into the puddles and
got covered with mud.

Back to their own house
they decided to go.

They sneaked in the window
so no one would know.

They put mud on the
carpets and mud on the beds,

Then crept under the duvet
and covered their heads.

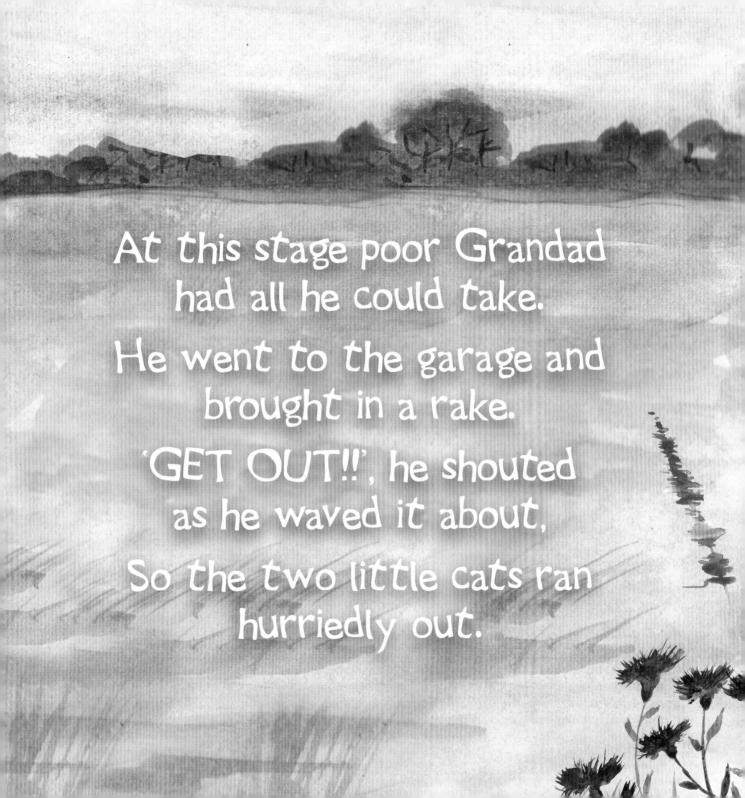

At this stage poor Grandad
had all he could take.

He went to the garage and
brought in a rake.

'GET OUT!!', he shouted
as he waved it about,

So the two little cats ran
hurriedly out.

They ran far away
as fast as they could,
And soon they were wet
and covered with mud.

They hid in the ditches
and felt very bad.

Both were very lonely,
homeless and sad.

Several days passed and
there wasn't a trace.

Without the two
cats it was a sad place.

Grandad was sorry he
had shouted that day.

He wished they were
back in the cottage to stay.

Then one sunny morning
he looked out the door,
The two little cats
were asleep on the floor.
He danced and he sang
with joy and delight.
It truly was an amazing sight.

To have them back home was
Grandad's great treasure.

He knew that the cats
would stay there forever.

Duchess and Valkerie
both live there still,

In that small country
cottage up there on the hill.

If you like this book, you'll love..

Available in book stores nationwide and online at doloreskeaveney.com